The Illegitima

©2020 by Molly Britton

All rights reserved. No part of this may be reproduced, distributed or transmitted in any form or by any means without prior written permission.

These stories are works of fiction. Names, characters, places and incidents are the product of the author's imagination and are used fictitiously. Any resemblance to events, locales or actual persons, living or dead, is entirely coincidental.

Chapter 1

Chapter 2

Chapter 3

Chapter 4

Chapter 5

Chapter 1

Eva Price was an imaginative sort of girl, the kind that preferred to let her mind wander far, far away from the cruel world she lived in. This was no surprise, considering the conditions she had been born into. As the daughter of Yorkshire's most prominent coal merchant, Nate Morris, any person might assume that Eva was bound to live a life of ease, one filled with fine china, piano lessons and dance cards. There were no petticoats and ribbons in Eva's life, however. Her father may have been a wealthy man, but her mother was no more than his servant who was turned out of his house as soon as her pregnancy could no longer be hidden.

At ten years old, Eva had never met her true father, but she dreamed sometimes about the beautiful love affair she assumed he had had with her mother. The truth was far from such a fairytale fantasy of course, but Eva let herself believe a different version of events. One where, perhaps, it hadn't been her father's fault her mother was turned out of the manor, and where, perhaps, if he met her, he would be so charmed by her, marry her mother, and they'd all live happily ever after.

"Tell me about my father," Eva would ask her mother sometimes.

"You know I have nothing to say about that man," Mary would answer.

"Did you love him?"

"In a way, but I shouldn't have. You, my dear, you are the only good thing that man ever made," Mary said, stroking her daughter's cheek.

"But he doesn't know I exist," she responded, repeating the words her mother had told her many times.

"And you're all the better for it, I promise you," Mary insisted.

"What about my grandparents? What are they like?" Eva pressed.

"I don't know what Nate's mother's name was. But his father was Henry, and he's an even crueler man than his son. He needed a cold spirit like that to build a successful business, but he never showed Nate any love."

Mary never liked to tell Eva anything of her father's family so as not to get her hopes up about pursuing a relationship with them. The reality of her connection with Nate had been a tragic one, and she didn't like to think of it. He had taken a liking to her the moment she'd started working at Longford Manor, as a lowly chambermaid. Having never worked in a fine household like that before, she'd been unsure of how to handle his attentions, although some of the other ladies had warned her about his behaviour. Mary had been flattered by the handsome, rich and charming master and believed him when he'd said he loved her.

She'd never told him of her pregnancy. The only person she'd opened up to was the housekeeper, trusting that she would help her. Instead, the housekeeper was scandalised by the realisation that one of her staff members was with child, and with the master's child at that. She told Mary that this was hardly the first time that a maid had fallen prey to Nate Morris, and it was positively unprofessional of her to have allowed the affair. Mary was thrown out of the house and told never to contact anyone at the manor again. For a few days, Mary waited for Nate to come find her, confident that his love was true. But he never did, and the stories the housekeeper had told her about Nate's other conquests swirled around her head. She made the decision then and there never to tell Nate about his child. He didn't deserve to know.

Once she was old enough to have learned where she came from, Eva just couldn't, or wouldn't, believe that her father was a bad man, choosing instead to indulge in a fantasy of misunderstanding. How could Nate Morris disown her as his daughter if he didn't even know she existed? Perhaps he had been looking for her all this time and simply couldn't find her. Maybe he'd never married another and was still in love with her mother. She dreamed of finding him someday and how he'd sweep her up, loving her the way a father ought to, and providing the safety she craved for both her and her mother.

Eva and her mother lived above a butcher's shop, the same shop where they both worked. Mary had married the butcher before Eva was born, and he was the closest thing she'd ever had to a father. Jack Price was as cruel as a stepfather could be. Although he had saved her mother from a lifetime of ruin as the unmarried mother of a bastard child, there was nothing charitable about him.

When Mary had worked at Longford Manor, she was often charged with running errands to the butcher's shop, where she met Jack. He had always held a candle for her, commenting on her bright eyes and opening the door whenever he saw her coming. His compliments made her blush, and he was kinder than most men, although not half as handsome as Nate. As soon as Jack had found out she had been thrown out of the manor and was in need of some assistance, he'd gone to visit her where she was staying at a boarding house, quickly running through the last of her wages.

"I know I'm not the best looking bloke, or the richest, but I've heard about your trouble, and I just wanted to say, I could… I could offer you at least a stable life, one with food on the table, and a roof over your child's head. And I could love you, in my own way," he said, bashfully. Mary was touched by his sweetness, although she was not particularly attracted to the man. He seemed to be a gentle man, with no knowledge of how to properly speak to women, but with a kindness in his heart.

"Do you really think you could care for me, as I am no more than a ruined woman?" she asked, eyes filling with tears.

"Of course. You are the prettiest, most wonderful woman I've ever met, and that man was a fool for throwing you away," Jack said, wiping a tear from her cheek and taking to his knee. He held her hand, looking up at her. "Mary, will you be my wife?"

At the time, Mary had seen his offer as a kind of salvation, a path towards a decent, and as he put it, stable life. As the child of paupers herself, long since deceased, Mary considered being the wife of a butcher to be a position far above anything she could ever hope for.

"Yes! Thank you, Jack, thank you. I will try to be the best wife to you I can possibly be," she said, and he kissed her gruffly. Despite everything, for a moment, she was happy.

They were married two days later, in a small chapel, with his brother serving as witness. She wore the only dress she owned, and a smile that no money could buy. As soon as the vows were sealed, there was a rude awakening in store for Mary, and nothing that Jack had promised her came to be. He was a drunk, and a violent one at that. Jealous and angry, he quickly let Mary know that he thought he'd done her a favour by marrying her, and she was nothing more than dirt. Having trapped her now, he forced her to work in the shop, but not in the front as she had imagined she would. Jack claimed he didn't like the way other men looked at her, so he kept her in the back, cleaning the blood off of knives and cold, metal equipment.

It was into these circumstances that Eva was born, and all she'd grown up knowing. Having learned to read herself, although most women of her station never learned the skill, Mary made sure that her daughter was taught well. There was never any hope of her going to school, but as soon as she learned her letters, Eva saw words everywhere, deciding she didn't need books if she could write them in her head. She was allowed no friends or toys, but the worlds she escaped to in her mind served as entertainment and distraction enough.

Jack saw in Mary a woman he could take advantage of and a pretty one at that, whose situation had rendered her helpless. In marrying her, he ensured that she would always be indebted to him, and he never let Eva nor Mary forget it. If she held her tongue, she could get through a whole day without Jack noticing her, but sometimes it was unavoidable.

"Get your head out of the clouds, girl. The cow isn't going to grind itself," Jack said, chuckling at his own words.

"Yes, Mr. Price," she murmured.

"I tell you what girl, if I was your father, you wouldn't have that streak of insolence in you. The Prices are a well-behaved family. What was your father but a lazy, rich, sorry excuse for a man? And I can tell, you are clearly his daughter."

Eva held her breath as she continued her work. Though she'd known the butcher shop her whole life and had been working there since she was old enough to turn the meat grinder, she'd never gotten used to the sight or smell of blood. The hanging carcasses turned her stomach on a daily basis, but Jack's ready fist and harsh words forced her hand. Even now, as most days, she had one yellowing bruise on her right wrist and fresh purple one on her cheek. As harshly as Jack treated Eva, it was nothing compared to the treatment he reserved for her mother.

There were days when Eva considered running away, though she had nowhere in particular to go. If only she could find her real father, she thought, everything might be different. He would see her, recognise her, remember his love for her mother, and everything could change. She had no way of finding him, however, and would more than likely end up in an orphanage, or returned to her cold-blooded stepfather. But the thought that truly kept her from running away was knowing what Jack might do to her mother if she wasn't there. There were nights when Jack got so blindingly drunk, he would beat Mary to within an inch of her life, and Eva feared that if she wasn't there to care for her mother, Jack might go too far. Eva would never forgive herself if that happened.

So she stayed, dreaming of a future when she could get away properly and save her mother from their miserable existence. Even if they only had a modest existence, it would be better than their current situation. There was a hint of promise that came when Jack fell ill, two years later. The coughing started on Eva's thirteenth birthday, and it was the best present she could have asked for, as dark as that seems. Crippled by illness, for two months Jack wasn't able to help out with operations at the butcher shop, leaving Eva and her mother to take over. Everything ran smoothly and as Jack could barely lift a finger, they were both spared his angry fist. Their newfound happiness couldn't last forever, though, and things changed when Jack's condition went from bad to worse. Though Mary cared for him, changing his sheets and feeding him by hand, as soon as he passed away, she and Eva were thrown out of their home. Jack's brother arrived minutes after the undertaker had taken away the body to announce that he was taking over operations of the butcher shop and that they had to leave immediately.

"I wouldn't want to call in the law, but I will, if that's what it takes," Jack's brother, Cecil, threatened, standing in the doorway and blocking all light coming into the modest room Eva and Mary shared.

"Please, Cecil, think of what Jack would want. He'd want you to show us some mercy. Let us stay the night, and we'll find a place in the morning. We know how to run the butcher shop, you can keep us on for half the pay, and we'll make sure that the business continues as usual. Of course you'll want to take over yourself, but let us show you the ropes and introduce you to the suppliers and farmers," Mary said, practically on her hands and knees. Cecil just watched the desperate woman, grinning.

"You ask me to think of what Jack would want? You think he didn't tell me how ungrateful you and your illegitimate spawn were? He did everything for you, and offered you everything, and you've let him die like this. I can't in good conscience let you stay," he countered.

"I did everything I could, I swear! But the doctor said, you can ask him, he said there was nothing more to be done but make sure he's comfortable. I beg of you, don't throw us out. Give me time to sort out another situation for us," Mary said, this time indeed falling to her knees, hands clasped together in desperation. The tears streamed down her cheeks.

"Don't waste your false tears on me, woman, I can see you for what you are - a clawing girl who will do anything to get what she wants. I have my own wife and child to think of. I can't be responsible for you as well. It's no fault of mine that you let Nate Morris have his way with you, and now you're in a spot of trouble. My brother had a heart of gold to take you in and marry you like he did, but I'm not so soft. You've brought this upon yourself, Mary. Now, take that grubby child and get out of here," he said, turning away.

Eva watched fearfully as something changed in her mother's face. An anger took over; anger at their circumstances, at the men who continually held them back and at the world for holding them down. She rushed towards Cecil, raining her fists down on his back, though he barely reacted.

"You monster, you! I bathed your brother, I spoon fed him and emptied his sick buckets. And what did you ever do to deserve his meager inheritance? What?!" she screamed, but Cecil only laughed at her plight. With one easy swipe, he pushed her off him, and she collapsed to the ground in tears. Cecil left them, to carry in the trunks he'd brought with all his belongings, ready to move in.

Eva and Mary had no choice. They took what they could, including bedsheets, and headed out to the streets before Cecil returned. They had nowhere to go, and no one to turn to. Mary had no other living family members, and at only thirteen, Eva had little to offer.

"Mother, what is the poorhouse meant for, if not for us? Can we not go there, and won't they help us?" Eva asked innocently.

"Trust me, my love, there is truly no worse place for us than the poorhouse. It's nothing more than torture. I'd rather us sleep in the open air than be taken to a place like that, where we'd be breaking stones and crushing bones," Mary insisted.

Hand in hand, the mother and daughter found a fairly comfortable place under a bridge, where at least they would be dry for the night. There, under the bridge by a small river, they lay in each other's arms, trying to keep each other warm in the cool night air. Eva tried her best to comfort her mother, but her tears were seemingly unending. Theirs was not like most mother and daughter relationships and sometimes, even at the tender age of thirteen, Eva felt as though she was the one taking care of her mother.

    The dreams and theories Eva had about her father had somewhat evolved over the past few years. Her current suspicion was that it was Nate's father, Henry, her grandfather, who had orchestrated Mary's expulsion from the household. Her mother had told her that Henry was a famously cruel man, and Eva thought that it was surely his plotting that had kept Nate from knowing of her existence, or

Mary's whereabouts. It was inconceivable to Eva that her father wouldn't help them if he knew of their dire circumstances. What kind of an evil man would deny his own flesh in a moment of need? She'd never voiced this theory to her mother before, as she knew Mary wouldn't take it well, but given how horrible their lives had become, and at no fault of their own, perhaps this was the moment to bring it up once more.

"Mother, do you think maybe that my father would be able to offer us some assistance? I'm sure that he would be terribly pained at the thought of us sleeping under a bridge. I could go to him and tell him of my true parentage. It could change everything for us," Eva said, getting excited at the thought, despite herself. Mary's tears had just started to slow, and she was exhausted from the emotional trauma of the day. Her daughter's midnight revelation was the last topic she wanted to discuss, if only because the thought of Nate always re-opened old wounds for her.

"Eva. We've spoken of this so many times. Yes, it's true that Nate Morris is not aware that you are his child, but I promise you my girl, he would not recognise you if you presented yourself to him, nor would he believe you. He would likely just think of you as a fortune hunter, hungry for his wealth. He's a greedy man, just like his father, with not a charitable bone in his body," Mary said faintly.

"Well what if you went to him? He certainly would not be able to refuse you, his old sweetheart. I'm very sure that he could never love another the way he loved you," Eva said naively.

"He's married now Eva and has been for quite some time."

The news was a bit of a shock to Eva who had always thought her mother knew nothing of what had become of Nate Morris. If she knew he was married, it meant that she had asked after him or, at the very least, someone had told her and she'd listened. Was this a sign that Mary still loved Nate, that she searched out news of him, and hoped as Eva hoped, that he would take them in once more? Of course it would be discouraging for her mother to have discovered he had remarried, but in Eva's thoughts, it only made sense. Of course he had found comfort in another woman. He likely thought that Mary was dead or long gone. How pleased and overjoyed he would be to discover she was still alive and had born his child!

Eva didn't bother her mother again that night but in her own mind, she hatched a plan. In the morning, she would seek out any knowledge of Nate Morris. If she could learn of her father's whereabouts, she would be able to announce herself to him, and all their troubles would be forgotten. Listening to the babbling of the river below them, and huddled next to the warmth of her mother, Eva enjoyed one of the deepest sleeps she'd had in months. Although they were without a home and had been reduced to begging, at least it was just the two of them now. There was no one to beat them for looking the wrong way or speaking out of turn. Jack was gone, and he couldn't haunt them anymore. They could make what they wanted of their lives, if only they could secure employment, or as Eva hoped more than anything, reach out to Nate Morris.

***

The morning was a clear one and Eva woke early, half out of excitement, and half due to the less than comfortable sleeping conditions. Mary rose with her, head aching from the rock they'd used as a pillow. There was nothing to eat for breakfast, but they washed themselves in the river.

"We'll walk into town. I'll venture to the tavern and see if they are looking for help and move along from there. I hate to ask, my dear Eva, but if you could beg passersby for anything at all, money or food, that would be a huge help. I promise we won't live like this for long. I hope you don't think me a failure of a mother," Mary said, tears threatening her eyes all over again, compounded by her exhaustion.

"Don't worry, Mother, I know the best spots for begging. I often see other children with their hands out, and I have noticed that strangers will be more likely to open their purses for the young than they are for the old. I'll do what I can. And don't for one minute think I don't love you, whatever our circumstances may be," Eva said, hugging her mother.

Of course, begging wasn't necessarily part of Eva's plan for the day. As soon as her mother left to seek work, Eva made sure she looked presentable, taking special care to rub all the dirt marks off her face and smooth down her wild, blonde hair. She'd have to make a good impression if Nate Morris was going to recognise her as his daughter. Eva hadn't ever met a rich man in person, but she rightly assumed that he would be more likely to accept her if she was presentable and well behaved.

Not knowing quite where to start, Eva walked to the magistrate's office, believing that there she might find someone who knew of her father. She'd seen rich and fancy looking people coming in and out of the building before and thought it would be the perfect place to start. It had occurred to her that if she found out where Longford Manor was, she would be able to go straight there and announce herself to Nate. As long as her evil grandfather, Henry, didn't get in her way, or if the manor was too far to travel to on foot, she would be able to finally meet her father as she'd always dreamed she would.

With her hair carefully braided and skirt as clean as she could get it, Eva stationed herself by the stairs at the magistrate's office, ready to ask the first gentlemen in a fine looking coat to come to her aid. She stood as straight as she could, knowing that fine ladies had perfect posture. Eva felt full of hope, as she did her best to be the prim and proper young lady she knew she was born to be.

"Excuse me," she asked a portly looking fellow who was looking at his pocket watch.

"No, I have no money for you girl, not even a farthing," he said, moving along past her as quickly as he could.

"I'm not asking for any money!" she called out after him, but he was too far away to hear her. It happened again and again, as gentleman after gentleman ignored her, clamoring to avoid the sight of her skinny and undernourished face.

Eva was not to be discouraged so easily. She changed her tactic and approached an elderly looking woman with a kindly face. She didn't appear to be quite as well off as the other people she had reached out to but she stopped, whereas not a single monocle sporting man had.

"Yes dear?" the woman said when Eva walked up to her.

"I was wondering, if it isn't too much trouble, do you know who Nate Morris is? Of Longford Manor?"

"Yes, of course I know of Nate Morris. I've never met the man, but everyone in these parts knows about the Morris family. Why do you ask?"

Eva shuffled between her feet before planting herself, remembering to be careful of her posture. "Well you see ma'am, he's my father, and I'm wondering just where I might be able to find him," Eva said carefully.

"*Your* father?" the lady asked, confused. Clearly, she was older than she even appeared. Eva made sure to speak more slowly this time.

"Yes, my father. I've never actually met him, but I'm hoping to go to Longford Manor this afternoon so I may meet him. If you could point me in the right direction…"

"You do look remarkably like his daughter, now that you mention it, but I believe you must be mistaken. Why, that's Nate, just there," the lady said, pointing down the road towards where a man was walking towards a carriage, holding the hand of a much younger girl. A girl about her own age, but even younger perhaps. "The poor man just lost his father, you know, and has the full run of the estate now. That's his daughter there. I've heard her mother is a legendary beauty, but she mostly keeps to the house. How do you…"

Eva dropped all pretence of politeness and ran off towards where her father was climbing into the carriage with the young girl. That was his daughter? Not only was he remarried to a great beauty, but he had another daughter, standing close enough to

Eva now that she could see her face. Eva stopped, stunned to see that her stepsister was almost identical to her. That was her family, it must be. The girl had dark brown hair, whereas Eva had the blonde hair of her mother, but that was the only difference between the two of them. It seemed to Eva that this other girl was a year or two younger than she was, but Eva had none of the expensive nourishment that she had, leaving her just as small. Her feet still glued to the cobblestones, Eva looked at the dress her sister was wearing, clean and a bright green with white lace around the collar, and a large bow around the back. It was the kind of dress Eva had only dreamed of and would likely never wear. Not unless she announced herself to Nate.

The carriage started moving, and Eva sprang into motion, chasing the carriage down the road.

"Wait!" she called out and the horses trod along, "wait, Father, wait!" The carriage was already moving too quickly, and they couldn't hear her. If only she hadn't stopped for so long to gawk at the girl. She felt silly for being so jealous of her sister when really she ought to have been excited that they were going to meet soon. She'd have her very own sister, and they were bound to be the best of friends.

Running after the carriage, Eva was spurred on remembering the words of the older woman. She'd told her that Nate's father had died which meant that Henry, the man responsible for throwing her mother out of

Longford Manor, could no longer keep her apart from her father. Everything was going just the way she dreamt it would, as long as she could keep up with the carriage. Eventually, she had to slow down, her legs stinging with the exertion, but the road was straight, and it didn't take long before she saw the manor appearing between the trees.

It was as large as her mother had said; an imposing grey building with a stunning fountain and garden in the front. Seeing it, Eva started laughing as she truly believed that all her troubles were about to be a thing of the past. She and her mother wouldn't be spending one more night under that horrible bridge. Yes, her father was married to another woman now, but he wouldn't be able to deny her once he saw the striking likeness between Eva and her sister.

Walking up to the front door, Eva stared up at the imposing entrance that would soon be her home. Working up her courage, she lifted the heavy knocker and brought it down, composing the words in her head that she would say to her father when he answered the door.

Only it wasn't her father who came to the door, it was a servant. A man in a tailcoat and neatly trimmed hair almost oiled down to his head.

"Servant's entrance is around the back," he said dismissively, closing the door almost as quickly as he had opened it.

"Oh, I'm not a servant. My name is Eva, and I'm the daughter of Nate Morris. Is he available to speak with me?" Eva asked in her most proper voice. The manservant blinked back at her, ingesting Eva's words.

"Who sent you here? Hattie is the master's daughter, and you are clearly not Hattie. We don't allow beggars on the property; you'll have to leave now! Shoo, off with you!" To Eva's surprise, he came outside and started chasing her away, down the entrance path as if she was an unwanted animal.

Unsure of what else to do, Eva started running away before the man finally stopped chasing her. Rushing past the matching hedges and flowing fountains that ran up the path towards the house, Eva ran and ran until she reached the imposing gates to Longford Manor. Slowing down once she returned to the road, Eva took in what had just happened.

How could she have been so stupid? She wanted to kick herself for her ignorance and innocence. Of course it sounded beyond ridiculous that she was Nate Morris's daughter. How could anyone believe such an outlandish story? She appeared like nothing more than an imposter and a beggar, hoping to trick the rich master of the house out of a silver candlestick or two.

Though she'd already run so far that day, she started sprinting down the road, getting as far away as she could from that menacing house. No one from the Longford staff would ever believe her story; after all, it was the housekeeper who had thrown Mary out in the first place. The pain of the realisation, and embarrassment at the scene, sent tears springing to her eyes, and she promised herself that she would never tell her mother of her foolishness that day.

Chapter 2

Eva went back to the spot in the town square where the other beggar children congregated. She was too tired to approach anyone and, waiting for her mother to come find her, watched as the pickpockets did their business. She hoped Mary had had more luck finding work than Eva had had pleading for pennies. If she tried now, she could probably manage to talk a few passersby out of a farthing or two, but the events of the day had simply been too much for her.

True, it had been the manservant who had turned her away from Longford Manor and not her father, but Eva couldn't help but worry that everything her mother had ever said about Nate was true. Perhaps he was a heartless man, and even if he was aware that she existed, living in the very same town as he, he would deny her the way his servant had. Considering it now, she hadn't liked the way he had grabbed Hattie's arm, and he was clearly not a charitable man. No one with a carriage and a house that grand ever gave a thought to the poor. She should have listened to her mother long ago. Legs aching, Eva sat on the ground and let the pain of the day, and indeed of her entire life, wash over her. She'd truly believed that the death of Jack would mark a new beginning for them and that Nate Morris would emerge as their saviour. But there was no one to save Eva and her mother; they'd had to save themselves.

"Eva! Are you all right?" Mary asked, making her way through the crowd towards her melancholy daughter.

Eva jumped to her feet, not wanting to worry her mother, not with everything else that was going on. She had to put on her best face to support her mother and never let her know where she'd spent the day.

"Yes, I'm fine, just tired. It was a wretched sleep under that bridge. I'm so sorry I wasn't able to beg for any money! All the people I asked simply turned away. You've always said it, but now I know it to be true, all the rich are heartless," Eva said, quickly coming up with an excuse for her lack of progress that day.

"Of course they are. I'm so sorry that you had to do that, it's humiliating, I know," she said, smoothing back the hair on her daughter's forehead. "I shouldn't have asked you to, it's cruel to force a child into such a degrading act. Can you ever forgive me?"

"Mother! I would beg for bread and pennies every day of the week if it meant that you got a moment of comfort. How was your day? Were you able to find work?" Eva asked, grateful that her mother believed her.

"Yes. It's hardly glamorous, and more than a little dangerous. And the pay isn't much, but I start at the mill tomorrow," Mary said, and Eva felt a pang of anxiousness. The story of the death of a female mill worker just last week had made the rounds. The mill's turbine was unprotected by a guard rail on the second floor, and Sally Turner's skirt got caught in the swiftly turning shaft. She was thrown against a pillar and killed instantly, but the sight of her spinning skirts would not soon be forgotten by anyone in the town.

"Please be careful, Mother," Eva pleaded, "Make sure to tie your hair up tightly every day and keep your skirts close to you."

"Don't worry, I'll be very careful, as careful as I can be. The pay is meager, but I was able to get us a room on credit at the Sawyer boarding house. I know Mrs. Sawyer from long ago, and she was kind enough to let me pay later once I get my first week's wages. It's just one room, and it's small, but I think you'll like it a considerable amount more than you liked our under the bridge accommodations," Mary said, seeming awfully proud of herself for having accomplished so much in just one day. Maybe they'd be all right on their own.

"My my, aren't we the fancy ladies! Imagine, having a bed! Well I never," Eva said giggling, and the mother and daughter paraded down the main street towards the boarding house, finding enjoyment in their make-believe banter.

Arriving at the Sawyer house, Eva flopped onto the bed she would share with her mother and looked out of the small window over the street. Tomorrow would be different, she told herself.

"Well my dear, I've managed to secure work and a roof over our heads, but I'm afraid I haven't given a single thought to food," Mary said, resting herself on the room's one chair.

A pang of guilt rang through Eva. If she had spent even a moment asking for help in the square as she was supposed to, she might have scrounged enough together to buy an apple, or a bit of bread for her and her mother to share. Instead, she had wasted her time and energy running after a carriage and embarrassing herself in front of a servant that would hopefully forget the sight of her face completely.

Suddenly, she thought of the way that girl, her sister, *Hattie*, had looked with perfectly braided chestnut hair with her ribbons and cold blue eyes. How was it that that girl, who looked so much like her, with their matching heart-shaped faces and small chins, how was it that she got to live a life of ease and leisure while Eva was in a cramped room, sharing a bed with her mother and trying to ignore the sharp hunger pains in her stomach? Was there nothing fair about the world at all?

"I'll go ask Mrs. Sawyer if she has anything left over from dinner, even any scraps she is going to throw out. She'll take pity on me, surely," Eva said wisely, knowing that her youth was a gift in this department.

"Thank you my sweet child. I don't know where I'd be without you," Mary said, kissing Eva on the forehead. It was a kind thing to say, although in her worst moments, Eva could help but think her mother might have been far better off without her. If she hadn't gotten pregnant with Eva, Mary might still be working at Longford Manor and likely, she never would have had to marry that awful man Jack simply to maintain her reputation. She shook off thoughts like that however, knowing that they were useless to dwell on. Perhaps her mother might have married Jack regardless and been in precisely the same position, with or without Eva having been born.

The young girl went down the stairs towards Mrs. Sawyer's room, knocking gently on the thin wooden door. Mrs. Sawyer lived by herself, her husband having passed away many years now, and she was a kind but stern woman. Running a business was no easy task for a single woman, and she'd learned early on to build a thick skin.

"Yes child?" the imposing woman asked when she came to the door.

"Mrs. Sawyer, I know you've already shown my mother and I so much charity and mercy, but I was wondering, we have nothing to eat, do you think you might have a scrap or two I might chew on? My mother doesn't know I'm here, she wouldn't want me to have bothered you," she artfully lied, "but the pains in my stomach are too great, and I'm aching for even the smallest bit of food."

Mrs. Sawyer looked down at her, and Eva couldn't tell what her implacable face was thinking. Was she about to get a slap across the mouth, or an embrace? She waited in silence for Mrs. Sawyer to say something more, but nothing was coming. Eva opened her mouth, feeling the need to fill the silence, but she had no idea what words to use. Suddenly and wordlessly, Mrs. Sawyer turned away and went towards the inside of her chambers, but left Eva standing there with the door open. Eva stepped into the room, assuming that perhaps she was meant to follow the woman, before instantly thinking better of it, and stayed in her place. A few minutes went by and finally Mrs. Sawyer returned, plate in hand with a bit of gruel, bread and cheese on it.

"Bring the plate back. And don't go thinking this will happen again. You can tell your mother it was my idea, I wouldn't want you getting into trouble now," Mrs. Sawyer said, handing Eva the plate before swiftly closing the door in her face. Struggling not to eat all of it before bringing the food back to her mother to share, Eva made a promise to herself.

The next day, she would try one more time to appeal to her father. She'd given him the benefit of the doubt for all these years; it wouldn't do to lose faith in him so soon, just because of the actions of one of his servants. The fact remained that Nate Morris had not a clue that Eva had ever been born, and she couldn't know what he would think before she'd even revealed herself to him. The only question that remained was how exactly she expected to find a way through to him. Always behind a veil of servants and maids positioning themselves like a guard around him, she'd have to catch him unaware. This would be the last time she would try such a stunt. Asking for food like that from Mrs. Sawyer felt extremely shameful. If this last attempt did not work, she'd have to move her dreams along, and focus on keeping her and her mother fed, by ways other than begging.

Eva and Mary shared the meager plate of food, and all traces of any crumbs were gone in minutes. They slept soundly that night, knowing all that needed to be done the next day, and ready to face the world.

Eva spent most of the next morning, after walking with her mother to the mill for her first day of work, wandering about town, asking anyone who would listen where she might find Nate Morris. It occurred to her that she might just go to Longford Manor and find him there, but she had no answer for what to do once she got there. Not wanting to face a barrage of servants again, Eva anticipated that he might spend the day in town and that it would be easier to get his attention there, away from the large stone walls of Longford.

No one seemed to know where he was, although she did have one kindly woman hand her a penny which she clung onto. At the very least *something* had come of the day, and she'd be able to get a bit of food for her and her mother that evening. Hours passed, and afternoon was starting to turn into evening before she finally laid eyes on her father. He was coming out of the tavern, only a slight sway to his step, and she immediately recognised the posture of his shoulders and mop of blond hair from the day before. There was no carriage in sight, which told her that he'd likely just taken his horse into town. This was good news, as there wouldn't be any servants standing in her way now, and no Hattie to distract her.

Eva took her chance, racing towards him, planting her feet directly in front of the man. He swayed slightly, confused by the stance of the small girl in front of him who looked oddly familiar. Eva herself lost her words for a moment, although she'd practiced what she was going to say the whole morning over. Her hand went up to her face, feeling the cheek that looked so much like the one in front of her.

"Excuse me," he finally said gruffly, putting an arm on her shoulder to push her aside but the young girl held her ground.

"I need to talk to you, Nate Morris!" she said, in as strong a voice as possible, and it worked. He stopped, looking at her with bewilderment.

"What?"

"I need to talk to you. You are my father. My mother never told you about me, as she never got the chance. Her name is Mary, and she was a chambermaid at Longford Manor many years ago. She was turned out of the house after becoming pregnant with your child, and then I was born. We're in dire need of assistance, and I just knew you'd want to help us. You see…" she started to further explain, but the rich man interrupted her.

"You are no child of mine. I know no one by the name of Mary, and even if I did, I wouldn't condescend to pay any attention to fortune hunters and schemers such as yourself. Out of my way, girl!" he said roughly, finally getting his chance to push her away. She clung to his hand for a moment, protesting his rejection, but he flung her off, and she hit the ground hard.

Shocked, she watched as Nate walked confidently away to where his horse was tethered, riding off into the sunset without a care in the world for her. Shaking off the dirt from her skirt, Eva stood up and took care to give herself a moment before making her way back to the town square. She stared after her father until she couldn't see his horse anymore, and then finally turned away. Well, that was that. She'd given him as much of a chance as she could have, and he'd thrown her away in the same way that Jack had. He was no better than her stepfather, and any illusion she'd ever had to the contrary was shattered. Her mother had been right the whole time, and she ought to have listened to her, but she just had to make sure for herself.

Clutching onto the one penny still in her hand, she let the loss of the day wash over her. Never again would she try and reach out to that horrible man. The most devastating part now was that she had no dream to cling on to, only a dreary future of fighting for survival at every turn, and no answers as to how to care for herself and her mother any longer. The one positive thought that Eva could gather from this was that now there were no men in their lives to pin them down or hurt them any longer. It would make everything a little bit harder, but without the threat of violence at every turn, they would be able to walk more freely around the world, with their heads held high.

Chapter 3

Two years later, Eva learned the hard way that her deceased stepfather and estranged real father were not the only men who meant them harm, and not the only system keeping them down. At fifteen, Eva was wise beyond her years and had seen much of the horrors of life that most women twice her age hadn't. For six months now, she'd been working with her mother at the mill, and the physical dangers of the job were almost more of a concern than what they'd endured from her stepfather, Jack. Accidents happened on the job frequently due to an overworked and tired workforce, unsafe conditions, and cruel masters. Still, it was the only way for

Eva and her mother to earn a living wage so they stuck with it.

Day after day, Eva waited for the accident that would take her or her mother's life. None of this felt worth it, but neither had been able to find an alternative. The rusty machinery had crushed the limbs of many of Eva's friends, and she dreaded the thought that she could be next. The days were long, often lasting twelve hours, and the breaks were few. They were still living at the boarding house, in the small room where she shared a bed with her mother, relying on the kindness and cooking of strangers. Sometimes, for a break in the rent, Eva did extra chores around the building for Mrs. Sawyer, but they were frequently very close to not being able to afford the rent. Eva knew that for all the kindness Mrs. Sawyer had shown them, she wouldn't hesitate to throw them out of the boarding house the moment they fell behind in the payments.

So on they worked, with hundreds of other women, with downcast eyes simply trying to make it through the day. The owner of the mill, Mr. Sannigan, was a mean sort of fellow and didn't often visit the building except to inspect the lines. Eva suspected that he was more inclined to inspect the women than the machinery, but she kept her mouth shut whenever he was near. He had a sharp nose and steep lean in his back and was somehow both thin and fat at the same time, with a ring of dark hair encircling his head, though bald on the top. It was impossible to guess how old the man was as his face was free of lines but his voice had the authority of an elder.

One fateful day when he was visiting the mill, Eva was on her shift and dutifully stopped her work as he passed by, curtseying as he came near. She happened to have worn her clean apron that day and was looking slightly more put together than her mother beside her. The coal that was burned in the mill was starting to have an effect on Mary's breathing, and Eva worried that she wouldn't be able to work much longer, and that the same shortness of breath would happen to her before too much longer.

"And who might you be, Miss?" Mr. Sannigan asked, stepping towards Eva and lifting her chin with his finger.

"Eva Price, sir," the foreman answered for her.

"I see. And how old is she?" the owner asked.

"Naught but fifteen, sir."

Mr. Sannigan stared at her, looking her up and down, before proclaiming, "Take her up to my office, I'd like to have a word with her. Regarding her... attire," he said slyly. The foreman nodded sharply and grabbed Eva by the elbow, dragging her towards the stairs to the side of the main floor. Before her head was whipped around, Eva exchanged a terrified glance with her mother. She had never seen this happen before to anyone else and had no idea what was about to become of her.

Forcing her up the stairs, the foreman taunted her, too quietly for Mr. Sannigan to hear, quite a ways behind them. Eva's heart was racing with fear. The foreman opened the door to the main office, shoved her inside and locked the door behind him. Frightfully, Eva struggled with the door knob, realising she was locked inside, and her breath quickened. Turning around, she looked around the office. There were large bookshelves surrounding a huge desk, all in the same deep, ominous mahogany. The desk itself was almost clear of anything at all, housing only an inkwell, quill, and stack of writing paper.

Before she could think what to do next, Mr. Sannigan was inside the office with her, clicking the lock shut behind him. She turned around, trying to think of what to say, or what on earth he wanted to see her about.

"Miss Price, I take it?" he asked, a sneer forming on his face as he pulled a chair out for her to sit in. She took it quietly, but he remained standing in front of her, just a short distance away, leaning against the back of the imposing desk.

"Yes, sir," Eva answered, continuing, "Apologies if my appearance today is below expectations, I…"

"On the contrary," he interrupted. "I wanted to commend you for your professionalism. So many of you women come into this mill dirty and wretched, reeking like the boarding houses you all live in. But you, you smell of something sweeter, and your bright eyes are a sign of health and happiness. All the mill women should strive to look as you do," he said, and Eva cringed, hating that he could recognise her smell. Her bright eyes were wet with tears, not health.

Young as she was, Eva was still unsure as to what this man might want with her.

"Thank you, sir," she said cautiously.

"I wanted to reward you for your fine work," he said, with a smile that did not rest well on his face. Was he trying to charm her?

"I thank you again, sir," Eva answered, wondering how exactly he meant to reward her.

"I understand that your mother works in the mill as well, is that right?"

"Yes, yes it is."

"Well. I should like to give you both a raise. I know it's challenging work that you do here, and I commend you for it." Eva just stared at him. Did he truly mean to pay her more simply for looking relatively well put together?

"Th…thank you, sir," she stammered, speechless. He laughed, and it was not a kind laugh. She could see now that he was young, no more than five or so years older than her, but he simply had the demeanour and cruelty of a much older man.

"You say that a lot, don't you Miss Price. 'Thank you,'" he teased.

"I'm…I'm not sure what else to say, Mr. Sannigan."

"Well, if you'd truly like to thank me, perhaps there is something you can do."

"Anything," Eva offered, and he pulled her up to standing. His hands were soft, but there was something menacing about his grasp. Without a second's notice, he tugged her towards him, holding her lips against his and clutching at her skirt. She pushed him off, using all the strength she had, forcing his face away from hers, but he refused to let go of her.

"What do you mean, to refuse me like this?!" he asked, turning her around and pinning her against the desk. Desperately, she tried to crawl up onto the desk, doing anything she could to get away from him. She was about to call out for help when he placed a hand over her mouth, pulling her head back towards his. "I could save you," he said in a dangerously low tone, "I could make sure you never go hungry another day in your life, and this is how you repay me? Obey me, and I'll see to it that you're taken care of."

Not for a single second did Eva consider his threatening offer. She screamed into his hand and kicked her feet out, trying to make contact with him, but he was stronger than he looked. Finally, she reached out with her hands, clawing at his face and eyes. Though her nails were short, her scratching finally distracted him, and she felt his blood well up around her fingers.

With him finally off of her, she screamed until the foreman unlocked the door, and she pushed past him, running down the stairs to where her mother was waiting. Behind her, Mr. Sannigan stumbled out of the office, shouting after her.

"Don't you ever come back here, you scum, do you hear me! You and your mother are both fired! Get out of here and I don't ever want to see your faces again!" Eva could hear the strain in his voice. Everyone in the mill turned around to see what all the fuss was about, and an incredible sense of shame came over Eva. There wasn't a single person in that mill who couldn't guess what had just transpired. Mary took her daughter's hand, and the two of them made a rush for the front door.

Once outside, they continued running all the way to the boarding house and didn't stop until they were safely inside their room. Eva collapsed against the inside of the door, falling into a pile of tears. Her knees had stayed firm throughout the entire traumatic event but now that they were safely away from Mr. Sannigan and the mill, they gave out.

"Mother! I'm so sorry, I didn't mean to… he grabbed me and…" Eva started telling Mary between sobs, but Mary stopped her.

"You don't have to explain a thing to me, you poor girl. Just let me hold you and let's forget this day ever happened."

For years now, Eva had been a source of stability for her mother and now, it was her chance to lean on her mother. Mary held her sobbing daughter until she fell asleep, her own eyes open until the wee hours of the morning.

Mary didn't want Eva to feel any shame or guilt about the incident despite the fact that their fortunes lay on a razor's edge. Even missing a few days of work was the difference between being able to pay for their room or being given the boot. They both immediately left the boarding house in the morning, looking for work to start as soon as possible. Neither of them found anything by the end of the day, and the same went for the day after that, and the day after that. Before too long, the reality of their situation sunk in for both of them. They weren't going to be able to find an employer in time to make their next month's rent, and even begging Mrs. Sawyer wouldn't give them any grace time. They'd depended on her charity too many times now, and she wasn't going to give them any more chances.

Two weeks later, they found themselves under the very same bridge they'd slept under years ago. The sense of failure that they both slept with on a nightly basis was only made more intolerable by the fact that they had been there before. Eva had thought that without the threat of a stepfather's fists that their lives would be easier, but that hadn't helped them for long. The world was built to keep them down, and there was nothing they could do to pull themselves up.

Eva tried begging in the town square but she was older now and less likely to be on the receiving end of kindly people's pity. There were younger and needier looking children to care for, and most people looked at her as if she ought to be trying to make something of herself. One day, the local blacksmith, Byron Adams, saw her and came over to inquire as to her well-being, and that of her mother. She had seen him every once and a while at the boarding house when they were still living there, and he often struck up a conversation with her mother.

"Eva Price, what are you doing here begging?" he asked, pulling her to her feet when he saw her.

"Well, my mother and I lost our jobs at the mill…"

"Yes, I heard," he interrupted, sparing her the need to tell the story again. "There aren't many people who didn't. But I thought you would find other work quickly, considering how resourceful both you and your mother are. I admire the way you both work so hard to keep your heads above water," he said kindly.

"Well it seems that word travels fast, and most other employers around town had heard that we would be distracting, so no one has taken us on. My mother is still looking for work now, but short of leaving for another town, I'm not sure what we are to do. And what is to become of us," Eva said, feeling herself spill all her worries out to this man she barely knew.

"Of course. That's so horrible. I hate to hear of something like that happening to good people like you and your mother. Tell Mary to come see me tomorrow, I might have something that could help," he said, and Eva smiled for the first time in weeks. There were still compassionate people in the world after all, perhaps.

When Mary got back from going to see Byron, the blacksmith, the next day, Eva asked her a thousand questions all at once, assuming that he had offered her some kind of job at his shop or that, perhaps, he knew someone else who could hire them on.

"No, he didn't offer me work," Mary said, choosing her words carefully and speaking slowly.

"What do you mean? What did he have to give you that could help us then?" Eva asked, confused. Mary took a deep breath in before answering.

"He offered me his hand. In marriage. He wasn't sure what else he could do for us, but he has a home that we could share, and he would be able to put food on the table. Food every day. And we'd never have to worry about being out in the cold ever again. He even offered to let us sleep in his shed this evening, as it would be improper for us to share a bed before being married, but he hated the thought of us out here in the elements."

Eva sat down, thinking. She and Mary had both promised long ago that they wouldn't let another man come into their lives and harm them, the way that all of them seemed to do, one after the other. But Byron Adams seemed like a nice enough man, and it must be true that *some* men weren't the horrible people that her father and first stepfather were. Almost anything would be better than the bridge they currently called home.

"Can you trust him?" Eva asked, with a large amount of skepticism in her voice.

"I think so," Mary said, and Eva studied her mother's face. In a way, Mary was always more likely to trust men than Eva was, and Eva could never understand why. Given the way the world worked, they would simply never be elevated beyond their current circumstances if one of them didn't marry.

"Do you want to marry him?" Eva asked.

"I think I could. I could *want* to marry him," Mary responded, as if she was convincing herself of her own words.

"Don't accept his proposal just yet. Let me talk to Mrs. Sawyer. She knew him, and she'll know if he can be trusted."

"But Eva, we have nothing! I don't know how much longer we can live like this, with no food or shelter. Byron has offered us a way out, and I think I should take it."

"Wait. Promise me that you'll wait. I want us to be careful this time."

Mary did promise, and Eva went first thing in the morning to see Mrs. Sawyer. Never a woman of many words, Mrs. Sawyer didn't have much to say, but in one thing she was very clear - Byron Adams was a man to be trusted, as far as she knew. And she'd known him his entire life. He'd never been married before, which was strange considering his social standing in the town, but Mrs. Sawyer seemed to think it was simply because he'd never met the right woman. Until now.

Mary and Byron Adams were married only three days later, and even Eva had to admit that the occasion was a joyous one. It seemed to all present, including herself, that their fortunes had changed. Byron was a good man who was helping them out in their time of need and truly seemed to care for Mary. He paid her special attention and bought the two of them the first new clothing and shoes they'd had in years. Eva could have cried for joy, and she did, several times.

The first few months of their marriage were pleasant. The glow started to come back into Mary's cheeks, and for the first time in her life, Eva had the time to make use of her reading ability. There was plenty to do around the shop and the house, which kept both Mary and Eva busy, but it was a business that they could take pride in. Slowly however, something shifted in Byron. It was subtle, but came on steadily, a sense of distrust in both Mary and Eva. Like Jack, he often praised himself for "saving" them, and started questioning the women anytime they wanted to leave the house. He had very strict rules about when they needed to be home and would raise his voice in a frightening way if they were ever late. Oddly enough, he would apologise immediately after, but Eva couldn't help but be frightened by the behaviour. In his worst moments, Byron would call them both tramps, saying that he couldn't trust that Mary wouldn't throw herself around to any man that could offer her a meal.

The words were painful and caused a growing rift in the household. Eva knew that his cruel messages could turn to violence at any moment, and she was devastated to know that despite their caution, Byron had still turned out to be just as hateful as all the other men she'd ever encountered.

Everything went from bad to worse when Mary started to fall ill, just after Eva's seventeenth birthday. At first it was just a cough, but when the blood started staining her handkerchiefs, Eva knew something was very wrong. The doctors weren't very helpful, instructing her to rest, leaving Eva to run the household and spend long hours alone with Bryon. They were painful hours, filled only with silence and snide remarks from her stepfather. A month later, it became very clear that Mary was not going to get better anytime soon.

"Why isn't her fever cooling, Eva? Are you not caring for her properly? I work all day long, pouring over a hot fire to put the food on the table, and you can't even put a cool cloth to your mother's forehead?" The accusations were unfounded, but Eva took them wordlessly, not wanting to further anger Byron. "Do you have any interest in showing me your appreciation of everything I do for you? Everything I have done for you?" he asked pointedly.

"Of course, stepfather. Please tell me how I can help," she said meekly, wishing to avoid any and all conflict.

"Your mother can't fulfill her marital duties any longer, thanks to her illness. Our marriage bed is cold, and it's time you warmed it. You're old enough now, developed enough. It's time you paid your mother's debts since she is incapable of doing so," he said coldly.

"Bryon…" Eva said, looking up at her stepfather and begging him with her eyes not to make her do the inconceivable. If this was truly how he expected her to repay her mother's debts, as he so cruelly put it, then he was a worse man by far than Jack had been, or her true father, Nate. How could he even suggest such a thing?! Eva would have preferred him to hit her than to go through with what he was asking of her. "I can't," she said finally. A large part of her wanted to get up and run straight out the door and never look back, but she couldn't leave her mother in the hands of such a man. If he was capable of asking this of her, what might he do to her mother if Eva wasn't there to stop him?

"You can't? Or you won't?" he asked quietly.

"Both," she answered, quickly this time.

"Don't think I can't force you to give me what I am owed by marriage law. Would you prefer to be forced then?"

"No, please, I beg of you, don't punish me for what can't be helped. My mother is sick, and we both deserve your compassion. It's true, we'd be on the streets if not for you, and I can't thank you enough for opening your home to us. I'll do anything. Anything else, but not that," Eva cried out, the tears threatening to pour out of her eyes.

Byron sat back in his chair looking pleased with himself. "Anything else? Is that true? You'd do anything else?"

Eva was quiet for a moment, trying to think what else she might be tacitly agreeing to, but nothing seemed worse than what he was proposing. "Yes, anything else." It was a risk, but she had to take it.

"Well, today might be your lucky day. I think there might be an opportunity that would benefit us both. Long ago, your mother told me of your true parentage, and don't think I haven't noticed the similarities between you and your stepsister, Hattie. She looks a good deal healthier and prettier than you, but that can't be helped considering your upbringing."

"What is this opportunity you speak of?" Eva asked quickly, wanting to hear what Byron was going to force her into. She'd had enough of his insults for an entire lifetime.

"Aren't you an eager one? It seems that Hattie has been stolen from Longford Manor. Her carriage was set upon by bandits three days ago as she was on her way to visit some friends, and she hasn't been seen since."

"That's awful," Eva said, a pang of sympathy running through her for the sister she'd never met. It would be terrifying to be stolen away like that, likely in fear for her life. It seemed her bloodline was doomed for tragedy. Though Hattie grew up having everything that Eva didn't, she still had suffered, and was suffering right this moment, if she was even still alive.

"Yes, it's awful, but I'll tell you the wonderful part of all this. Nate Morris and his wife are posting a thousand pound reward for her return."

"What are you saying, Byron, do you know where she is? Was it you that took her from that carriage?!" Eva said, trying to understand why Byron would be so thrilled about a reward that couldn't possibly apply to them. Unless he had done something truly terrifying.

"No Eva, I didn't steal the girl myself. Is that what you think of me? You are thicker than I even thought. Eva, you are the spitting image of the girl, except for your blonde hair which we'll have to do something about. Don't you see? We can darken your hair, take you to Longford Manor where I'll collect the reward, and then you'll be able to live in the estate yourself as if you were a member of the family."

"I am a member of the family," Eva countered.

"Hardly. But I think we can pass you off as one easily enough. That's the correct spirit to have in this instance of course. I know you can read, write and sew. Could you mask your language to sound more mannered? You look thin of course, but that can be easily explained away as you have been theoretically starving for days with those bandits."

Eva did her best to poke holes in Byron's ludicrous plan, but it was clear he had thought it through. The parts he didn't think through were how she was expected to keep up this charade once they discovered that she had none of the manners of a fine lady. She had never learned to dance or play piano. How was she to explain all of that? The truth was that Byron didn't care what became of her once he had received the reward. It worried Eva that she would be leaving her mother in the hands of this madman, but it didn't seem like she had a choice. Byron had set his mind on it and offered her an impossible choice. Pretend to be her sister or share his bed.

That night, they set to the task of darkening her hair using coal tar, and the effect was surprisingly effective. Looking in the small mirror, Eva herself had to admit that she was the spitting image of her stepsister. Over the years, she'd caught glimpses of Hattie around town, and was always struck by their similarities, which were many. Byron had torn apart one of Eva's old dresses, making it seem as if it had been something the bandits had forced her to change into while she was held captive.

Eva made the decision not to tell her mother of the plan so as not to worry her. Regardless, Mary was too delirious with fever to realise what was happening anyway, so Eva simply kissed her mother on the cheek in the morning and tried her best to hold back her tears. Something told her that might be that last time she ever saw her mother. She couldn't trust Byron to treat her mother properly once he had secured the reward, but at the very least, he wouldn't be able to use poverty as an excuse for not taking care of her. He tried to assure Eva that he would bring her back to health himself if only she could do this one thing for her.

Without a single belonging with her, Eva was marched by Byron all the way to Longford Manor. It was an excruciatingly long walk, but Byron had insisted that the rescue would appear as more authentic if they arrived on foot. She considered telling whoever answered the door at the manor the truth before Byron could get a word in, but she thought better of it. Byron would be put to death if she told the truth, and then her mother would surely die alone. They couldn't survive another brush with homelessness. Without having produced an heir for Byron, his blacksmith's shop would become the property of some distant family member, and Mary would be kicked out into the streets once more.

Approaching Longford Manor once more, Eva remembered the last time she'd been there, years ago now. She was terrified, even more terrified than the last time she'd been standing on the same steps, but part of her was also excited, though guiltily so. Since she'd been a little girl, she'd fantasised about what her life would be like if she was recognised by her father and welcomed into the life that was taken from her. If she could pull it off, she was about to find out exactly what that life was like.

"Remember, I found you in the woods by the Wallace farm. What's your name?"

"Hattie Morris of course," Eva said in the perfect posh accent she'd been working on since the night before. It wasn't perfect, but hopefully no one would notice.

Byron knocked on the door, using the same large knocker she'd struggled to lift when she was but thirteen. A woman answered the door this time, a large and friendly looking housemaid who smiled when she saw Byron. He cleaned up well, having shaved and combed his hair. Indeed, Eva had to admit, he looked like an upstanding member of society.

"Yes, what can I help you with?" she asked politely, giving them a much different welcome than that rude manservant Eva remembered.

"Ma'am," Byron said, taking his hat off and bending his head, "Ma'am, I'm pleased to say that I've found…"

"Hattie?! Hattie is that you? What have they done to you, you poor girl?!" the woman said, pulling Eva into the grand entrance before Byron could even get another word in.

"Yes, yes it's me," Eva said, testing out her voice, and speaking quietly. Looking back at Byron, he nodded with approval. The woman, whose name Eva was clearly supposed to know, sprung into tears and clutched the young girl to her chest.

"I found her by the Wallace farm, just in the woods. She doesn't seem to remember much, but she missed you all terribly. I think that trauma has affected her head somewhat," Byron said, putting on a voice himself, a kind voice she remembered hearing when they first met.

"Thank you, thank you, sir, for returning her to us! Master!" she called into the parlour, "Master! Hattie's been returned to us, come see her!"

It was the moment she'd been waiting for her whole life. Nate Morris came running into the hall, took one look at her and swept her up into his arms. She'd never been held with such affection by anyone in her life other than her mother, but it was short lived.

"I must say Hattie, what have they done to you? You smell like a barnyard," Nate said, backing up several feet.

"This gentleman here found her by a farmer's field which explains the smell. They must have starved you, you poor girl, you look so thin. And these rags they've thrown you in! What a tragedy. Doesn't she look thin, Master?" the housemaid asked.

"She certainly does. You'll have to tell us everything that happened to you girl, but I beg of you, Laura, wash this girl before I grow nauseous from her smell. Or the sight of her. Come see me in my office when you are ready Hattie. Sir," he said turning to Byron, "Follow me. You must receive your reward as promised. I thank you for returning our girl. Do you have a daughter yourself? It's impossible to keep track of them. Sometimes, I think Hattie will be the death of me," Nate said, taking Byron with him down the hall. Eva hadn't been sure if Nate would believe

Byron, or if he'd think that he was the one responsible for her disappearance, but apparently it was easy for Nate to believe a man such as Byron. She hoped it would be the last time she saw her stepfather, but she couldn't be sure.

"Let's get you upstairs. I'll have a bath drawn for you, and then we'll get something in your stomach. You must be starving, but it's important to not eat too quickly, you hear me? I must say, you're awfully quiet, Miss Hattie. I don't like to think what they did to you to make you quite so silent. I suppose your tongue will return to you soon enough. You've been through quite a time after all," the woman chattered on as she led Eva up the grand staircase and towards what Eva could only assume was her very own room. *Laura*, Eva thought to herself. Nate had referred to this woman as Laura. She'd never had her very own room.

The upstairs hall was just as large as the downstairs one, and Eva stared up at the paintings that lined the way. Paintings and portraits of her very own family members, family that she'd never met, but now assumed she would. The ones who were alive at any rate. She made a mental note to study them later and learn all their names. She'd have a lot to learn if she was going to successfully make the entire household believe that she was Hattie, and listening and reading would be the key.

Laura opened the door at the end of the hall, and Eva was about to follow but she was momentarily distracted by a large painting to the left of the door. It was a portrait of Hattie, clearly done recently, and Eva couldn't tell the difference between the girl she was staring at and herself.

"Miss Hattie? Are you quite all right?" Laura asked, coming back outside to check on her. "Isn't it a fine painting? Mr. Ward did such a fine job. He'll be so pleased to hear of your return and will call on you soon, no doubt. Not to worry, we'll have you looking just like your old self long before Mr. Ward sees you," Laura said with a smile on her face.

Mr. Ward? Who was this man? Clearly not a relation, but a painter. A painter Hattie had some kind of a relationship with. Eva wondered if they were of a similar age, or if he was an older gentleman, a kind of mentor. *Did Hattie paint too,* she wondered? How many skills would she have to pretend to have lost in the past few days before someone started to suspect her?

Entering Hattie's room was surreal for Eva. Everything was a pristine white, and the four poster bed was the biggest bed she had ever seen. Wandering around, she wanted to touch everything. There, on the vanity, was the finest set of ivory combs Eva could have imagined. She caught sight of herself in the framed mirror, and thought she looked awfully out of place with all the finery surrounding her.

"The hot water is on the way up now. Why don't you rest for the moment, and we'll have you cleaned up soon. Give me your rags, I'll have them burned in the kitchen," Laura said, holding her hands out for Eva to hand her the clothes she was wearing. Stunned for a moment, but quickly coming to, Eva undressed herself and handed over her stained grey dress, taking the shift Laura was holding over her head. It was soft, softer than anything Eva had ever worn.

"Catherine will be up in just a few moments to help you get cleaned and dressed. I'll see you in the dining room as soon as you're ready, and then we'll take you to see your father," Laura said before leaving the room and closing the door behind her.

Eva sat on the bed and waited, staring out the window over the green fields and forested grounds of Longford Manor. She wanted to cry, desperately sad that her mother wasn't here to experience all this with her, but was instead languishing away with sickness in

Byron's smoke-filled home. It seemed to take forever for the bath to be filled, and in the meantime, Eva looked around the room, opening drawers and looking at all the fine clothing that belonged to Hattie. Underneath some of her underclothes, she felt a book, and pulled it out. It was Hattie's diary. This was an incredible find, and could be the key to Eva successfully managing the ruse she'd gotten herself into.

Leafing through the diary, lined with names she didn't recognise and would have to learn, Eva noticed that about two weeks before Hattie had gone missing, the diary entries stopped. She stopped on a page that mentioned Luther Ward, the same Mr. Ward who had painted the portrait of Hattie.

Father seems to think he'd be a good match for me, and yes, he's nice enough, but it's difficult to imagine spending my entire life with someone like him. Son of the only other wealthy family in the area, I do concede that the connection would be a wise one, so I'll try to make the most of our time together. Laura says that men and women can grow to love each other, even if they don't have a spark from the start. He's to start painting my portrait next week.

How I wish mother was still alive to guide me in this regard. How is a girl supposed to make her way in the world without words of wisdom from her mother?

"Miss, your bath is ready. Come this way," Catherine said, leading her towards the adjoining room with a big brass tub in the middle of it. Eva put the diary away quickly and followed Catherine. Settling down into the tub of warm water, and feeling Catherine's sponge cleaning her arms and back for her, Eva tried to keep her hair from getting wet, fearing that the dye might run if it did.

She thought of the words in the diary again. Luther Ward was clearly courting Hattie, and Hattie wasn't quite sure how she felt about him. Eva couldn't blame her sister for being skeptical of marriage. After all, Eva had witnessed two examples of just how bad it could go. She wondered how it was for Hattie's mother and Nate. Then she remembered - Hattie's mother was gone, dead she had to assume. It would be so lonely in this big house without a mother or any sisters.

Looking up at Catherine, Eva wondered if she was friends with Hattie. Ought she to be speaking to her familiarly? How did one usually communicate with the staff? She thought it best to keep quiet for now until she could observe more.

"What would you like to wear, Miss Hattie?" Catherine asked, and Eva froze.

"Would you pick for me, please?" she asked, saying the only words that came to her mind.

"Of course. I think the green and white would do nicely for your return. May I say, Miss, it's very nice to have you back. And I'm sorry for everything that's happened to you," Catherine said, pulling the laces on Eva's corset tight and fetching a forest green gown for her.

"Thank you. It's very nice to be home," Eva said carefully. Catherine reached for a comb to start working on Eva's hair, but Eva stopped her, again worried about her colour coming out on the comb.

"I'll do my own hair. If you don't mind. It's odd, I know, but I think it's what I'd prefer," she said, and Catherine silently handed over the comb. The last thing Eva needed was Catherine noticing any of her hair colour coming off on the comb.

As soon as she was presentable, Eva made her way down to the dining room, where an extravagant meal was waiting for her. Fine cheese and fruits, and other sweets made of beautifully coloured sugar. She wasn't quite sure where to start, but once she did, she couldn't stop. It wasn't until Laura suggested that she might have had enough that Eva realised she needed to slow down. Luckily, Hattie's "starvation" served as excuse enough to explain her ravenous behaviour.

Then it came time to speak with her father. Eva didn't know which way to go and half considered just wandering around the manor until she found his office, until she thought better of it.

"Laura, will you walk with me to father's study? I simply cannot bear to be alone at the moment," Eva said, using a voice slightly higher than her own natural tone. Laura just stood and blinked for a moment before speaking once more.

"Of course, of course I will. Shall we?" she asked, pointing towards the hallway. Eva slowly ventured towards it. They walked together, as Eva carefully followed Laura's directional cues until they were in front of a dark, thick oak door. Eva stepped forward and knocked on the door, tentatively at first, before she gained her confidence and knocked harder.

"Come in," her father called from inside, and she opened the large door. Laura waited until she was inside to go back to her other duties.

Once inside, Eva thought that her father's office looked remarkably like Mr. Sannigan's office at the mill. The same large, dark bookshelves and mahogany desk. Only whereas Mr. Sannigan's desk had been almost empty of objects, her father's was covered with papers, quills, letters and small trinkets.

"There's the Hattie I remember. How are you feeling? Better?" he asked, as Eva sat down across from him.

"Yes, I'm still quite shaken up, but feeling better. It's odd, I feel as though the trauma of the event has damaged my memory," she said, trying in advance to explain any mistakes she might make.

"I can only imagine. So, tell me. What happened? Who were these bandits, and what did they do with you?"

Eva took a deep breath. She'd been preparing for this moment. "I only remember flashes. Their faces were covered, the bandits, so I don't know who they were. And then they blindfolded me and drove the carriage away to who only knows where. It was dark where they were keeping me, and honestly, Father, between the tears and hunger, I don't remember much at all. Then they left me in that field after, I assume, they'd taken everything they could have from the carriage. Hopefully, more will come to me in time, and we'll be able to apprehend those responsible," Eva said carefully, working up some tears to colour her story.

It seemed to work. Nate was clearly uncomfortable with this display of emotion from his daughter. It somewhat surprised Eva, but it shouldn't have, that Nate's relationship with his daughter was quite distant. If it had been her that was newly reunited with her mother, Mary would have held her close for hours. Nate, on the other hand, looked as though he was in a business meeting he wished would end.

"I see. And what became of the driver?" he asked.

"I did not see. For all I know, he might have been in on it," Eva said, shifting the blame and suspicion elsewhere. Nate looked thoughtful, and they were quiet for a moment.

"Well, I am blessed to have had you returned by that kindly man, Byron. Your mother would never have forgiven me if I had lost you like that. Losing her was already more than I could abide." For a moment, Eva thought that Nate might cry, but he quickly composed himself. "I sent word to Luther that you were safely found, of course. I suspect he will come and see you as soon as he receives the message, possibly tonight. This incident may be worked to our advantage. Perhaps your disappearance will have further confirmed his love for you, and we can expect a proposal any day now. It's the least we can hope for, considering how incredibly expensive it was to save you. Girls like you cost a pretty penny," he said, looking at Eva as if she ought to be thanking him for posting a reward she never asked him to. She did anyway.

"Thank you for all your efforts to recover me, Father. I'm sorry for the great cost," she said, bowing her head. The rest of their meeting passed quickly and afterwards, she went straight back to her room, where she read Hattie's diary cover to cover, learning all she could about Luther and her sister's life. Nate had agreed that she might skip tea and dinner if she wished, and take the time to recuperate in her room. He mentioned again that it was likely Luther would call, given his affection for her, and Eva wanted to go into that visit with as much information as possible.

Nate had said that he was expecting a proposal any day now, and indeed, according to Hattie's diary, she was as well. It was unclear whether or not Hattie cared deeply for Luther, but at the very least, she seemed to be going along with the match for the sake of her father and his business. Eva had a sneaking suspicion that Hattie had been censoring what she wrote in her journal for fear of it being discovered. Still, it was a fantastic resource for her and would help greatly.

Luther did call, shortly after dinner time, and Eva was summoned down to the parlour to meet with him. She smoothed her hair and dress, looking once more in the mirror at herself. Though she missed her mother dearly, there was something thrilling about this adventure. Eva hadn't met a decent man in her whole life, but part of her was looking forward to meeting Luther. If he could paint a portrait like the one hanging outside of her room, so full of soul and heart, it must have meant he was a different sort of man.

"Hattie," he said when he saw her, rushing forwards and kissing her hand. He looked as if he wished to hold her close to him, but propriety was holding him back. Eva looked him over. He was tall, with deep brown, curly hair and dark circles around his eyes that betrayed his worry to Eva. Clearly, he cared about Hattie, and was distraught at her disappearance. "I hardly even know where to begin. I've missed you so. I've been up all hours of the night thinking of where you might have disappeared to. I can't tell you how relieved I am that you've been returned," he said. His gaze struck something deep inside Eva. Though she had her reservations, something about this man seemed trustworthy. "How are you?"

"I'm doing as well as can be expected," Eva answered, more nervous in front of Luther than she had been with anyone else. Laura was in the room with them, serving as chaperone, as Nate couldn't be bothered and there was no one else in the household that would be appropriate.

"I should like to know what happened, but I don't wish to force you to speak of uncomfortable topics. I expect you've told the story several times over by now," he said as they sat together on the uncomfortable, but beautiful, chaise.

"I have. If you don't mind, I would like to speak of other subjects. How have you been filling your days since I last saw you?" she asked, trying to turn the conversation back towards him. In her experience, men loved to speak of themselves.

"I've done nothing of note, and I haven't been able to paint at all. Father's been trying in vain to talk of the business with me, but I just couldn't focus, my mind was only thinking of you suffering out there at the hands of those bandits. I apologise, I don't mean to bring it up again. I meant to bring you something to comfort you, but I come empty handed. Is there anything that I might bring to you tomorrow, to ease your suffering?"

"I'm not quite sure. Perhaps some reading material? I should like to read some distracting novel. Something to replace the wretched memories with," Eva said, saying the first thing that came to her mind. It was true that she would like something to read, having never before been in the position to make use of that skill. Books had never been affordable for her and her mother, although she craved the escape they might be able to provide her.

"Books? You'd like a book?" he asked, looking surprised, and Eva panicked. Had she said the wrong thing?

"If it's not too much trouble. Of course…"

"It's no trouble at all," he interrupted, "Only, you've never shown any interest in reading before. So I'm curious as to what's brought it on." Something in his eyes changed, and Eva could tell. Quickly, she came up with an explanation.

"I'm not sure, but I suppose something about this experience has changed me. I find the idea of conversing with other people to be quite frightening, present company excepted of course. Books seem as if they might present a welcome escape." Looking at him, Eva hoped that he believed her. His eyes held her gaze, and her breath quickened.

"Well then, books you shall have, as many books as you desire. I've long wished to have someone to discuss the latest novels with, and I see now I shall have the opportunity. More than that, I shall bring you distractions. We shall never speak of this horrible experience again."

They spent the next hour talking. Eva felt she needed to guard herself, lest she say the wrong thing again, though being in Luther's presence made her feel relaxed as she'd never felt in the presence of a man before. Of course, he couldn't be trusted just yet.

For Luther, he left that evening with a smile on his face, promising to return the following day with distractions a plenty for his Hattie. On his way home, he considered the evening. Something about her demeanour was odd, although he couldn't quite place what. And for that matter, there was something in her look that wasn't quite as he remembered. The line of her nose was shallower, and her cheeks wider than the Hattie he knew. Having painted her portrait, he was well aware of her edges and curves, and this girl was different. There wasn't enough information to go on just yet, however, and he'd need more time to make an accusation. He resolved to spend as much time with her as possible, even more time than he had previous to her disappearance, so he might get to the bottom of the mystery.

True to his word, Luther arrived the next day with a case full of books and everything they would need to play croquet.

"There's nothing quite like a rousing afternoon of lawn games to get your mind off things, don't you agree, Hattie?" he asked as they found an appropriate bit of grass to set up on. The garden and grounds at Longford Manor were stunning, and Eva had wanted the chance to explore them.

"I absolutely agree," she said, though she knew none of the rules. "You'll have to remind me how to play the game. I'm afraid that the rules have completely slipped my memory. Another effect of the incident, I believe."

"Why, we played only two weeks ago, right here in this very same spot!" he said, and Eva panicked. Using her worry to her advantage, she didn't try to stop the tears that sprang to her eyes, and Luther instantly melted, apologising for his behaviour.

"Of course, I do apologise for upsetting you. Look here, I'll do a little dance to cheer you up," he said, starting to jig around the lawn. Eva doubled over in laughter, for the first time in recent, and not so, recent memory. They passed the rest of the afternoon joyously, playing several rounds of croquet and reading to each other in the sun, followed by a lively discussion of the material.

Eva, quite truly, had never been so happy in her entire life, though she felt incredible guilt in thinking that. Her mother was still suffering, and she had no way of getting word to or from her. Here she was laughing away the sunny day, while the only person she cared for in the entire world was trapped. Eva shuddered to think how Byron was treating her now. It would only be a matter of time now before he wrote to her and asked her to send money, though she didn't know the first thing about how to get any. She was growing accustomed to life around the house, but the idea of travelling into town and meeting new people filled her with anxiety. It would only take one wrong move for someone to notice her true identity, and she'd spend the rest of her life rotting away in a prison, or forced into factory labour.

Perhaps however, if she did marry Luther, she would be able to carry on the ruse, and bring her mother to live with them, posing as a nursemaid for her future children or the like. It seemed as though Luther trusted her and did not suspect her true identity. More than that, he seemed to *like* her. And she liked him. Though the notion of being forced into a marriage was repugnant to her, perhaps a marriage to Luther would not be so terrible. She'd seen the way Byron had become a terrible husband, however, so she would not be quick to believe Luther's integrity until they had spent more time together. For now, he was a valued friend, her only friend, and she looked forward to him coming back the next day, and the day after that. Her father clearly did not care what she did with her days as long as she stayed on the grounds for her own safety, so she was free to do as she pleased around the house. It was empty without Luther's presence, and she longed for his company when he was absent.

So it was that Luther spent the better part of each day for a week in Eva's company, and the two grew quite close. Unbeknownst to Eva, Luther left each day with more and more certainty that the girl was not who she said she was, yet he could never quite bring himself to confront her. With the old Hattie, he'd grown infatuated with her beauty, but the conversation was nothing like his conversations with this new Hattie. "New Hattie," as he'd come to call her in his mind, had all of old Hattie's beauty, but a deepness to her that he adored. She offered perspectives he'd never considered before, yet there was an innocence to her that was wonderfully charming. It pained him to think of why she might be lying to him and to the entire Morris household, but every time he considered her motivations, the perfection of her face and laugh took away any of his bitterness. He was letting himself be distracted by this new Hattie, justifying her actions, and in turn, his affection for her. Of course, there was a time limit on their friendship, as eventually he'd have to confront her with the truth, but for now, he let it go.

For in truth, new Hattie was the bright spot in his life. Luther was the heir to a tremendous fortune, and his father wished for him to take over the business, but Luther was not in the least bit business-minded. He tried to tell his father over and over to hire another man to run the company in his absence if he wished to retire so badly, but his father balked at the notion that anyone but a Ward family member would be the head of the company he'd worked so hard to build. Painting was Luther's passion, though his father considered it a silly distraction from his real work and disapproved of the undertaking.

As soon as the new Hattie revealed her true identity to him, he'd have to break off the acquaintance, and the courtship, going back to a colourless life of arguing with his father. So he continued on, spending as much time with new Hattie as he could, enjoying what would surely be a short lived dream.

The day that it all came to an end, Luther was in a less than playful mood, following another argument with his father, and Eva could tell there was something weighing on his mind. It was a rainy day, and they had taken over the parlour, playing a sullen game of old maid.

"It's your turn, Luther," Eva said, as Luther stared out the window, looking at the raindrops pattering against the glass.

"Hmm?" he responded, turning back towards her slowly.

"It's your turn."

"Right," he said, slowly looking at his hand again.

"Luther, tell me what's on your mind. I can tell that you are distracted," Eva said, putting down her cards. She'd never seen him looking like this, a sadness in his eyes that ran a thousand miles deep. He was quiet at first, but put his cards down as well, signalling that he wanted to confide in her, but wasn't quite ready.

"I had another argument with my father," he said, when he finally spoke.

"What about?" she asked, though she could guess.

"What we always argue about. He thinks I'm wasting my time with all this painting nonsense, and wishes for me to get more serious regarding the family business. He doesn't understand why I want to travel and work on my art when I could be dedicating my time to growing the company, and building the family fortune. And I'm starting to agree with him," he said, looking down and avoiding Eva's eyes.

"No, don't say that," Eva protested. She had grown to love all of Luther's work, including, of course, the beautiful portrait of Hattie that he had done, hanging just outside of her room. With their usual chaperone, Laura, temporarily out of the room, Eva took the opportunity to reach for his hand. He took hers gratefully in his, and her heart beat faster feeling the warmth of his skin against hers. "Your paintings are incredible, and your father must recognise that you have a gift, family business or no family business."

"I know, but as the sole heir, it is my duty to take over, and I've been putting it off for long enough. He also wishes that I would stop spending so much time courting you. Not that he doesn't approve of the match, but he wishes that it was already secured. Of course, I don't want to rush into anything as I know that you're still recovering from your traumatic experience. I've loved spending this time with you this week Hattie, and I… I…" he trailed off, still holding her hand, eyes lost in hers. He so badly wanted to tell her everything on his mind, but as soon as it was revealed that she was not who she claimed to be, he would have to cut off all contact with her, and that brought him immense pain. "I care for you deeply Hattie, I want you to know that. Whatever happens, don't forget that."

Eva sat quietly, ingesting the information. She could feel his affection for her, and her heart felt the same tenderness, though it was also filled with sadness. She could not allow him to fall in love with her without telling him the truth. There was no telling how he would react when she revealed the deception, but they could not go on like this any longer.

"Shall I call for tea?" Laura asked, coming back into the room, and the pair quickly pulled their hands apart.

"No thank you, Laura," Eva said, thinking quickly, "I think that we should like to take a walk outside. Wouldn't we, Luther?" she said, looking straight into his eyes and trying to communicate her intentions to him. Walking outside was the only way they might be able to continue this conversation unencumbered by the prying ears of Laura. He understood and went along with the scheme.

"Yes, I'm afraid I'm getting quite overheated in this stuffy room, with the fire. It's a tad smoky, don't you think?"

"But it's raining. Surely you don't mean to take a stroll in such miserable weather," Laura said, looking confused.

"We'll take an umbrella. You needn't come with us Laura, if you don't like it. We'll stay just out front there, so you'll be able to see us," Eva said, standing up so as to stop Laura from protesting. Luther followed suit, and they moved towards the front entranceway as Laura rushed to bring them an umbrella. It was painfully quiet as they waited, each not wanting to ruin the fantasy they'd been playing at for the last week.

The doorman opened the imposing front doors, and Luther held the umbrella over them both as they solemnly made their way outside. Finally, out of earshot of any of the servants, they both went to speak at once. They laughed nervously, before Luther kindly allowed Eva to say her piece.

"I wanted to say… I want to say a great many things. But firstly, I want to say that I care for you too, deeply. As you say, whatever happens, please believe me on that accord. I need to tell you that…"

"Don't. Please just let us stay as we were…"

"I can't go on like this. I have to be honest with you. I cannot stand idly by as our connection grows without telling you who I am. But believe me, I am disclosing my truth to you specifically because of the tenderness I feel towards you." Luther braced himself for the truth, looking towards the large oak tree they were standing under. Any pretence of a walk had been lost. Laura was looking out at them from the parlour window, but it was impossible to tell what she thought they were talking about. Eva took a deep breath. "I am Nate Morris's daughter. But I am not the daughter of his former wife, nor is my name Hattie. My name is Eva Price, and my mother was a servant here, many years ago. She and Nate had an affair, an affair of which I am the product. As soon as it was clear that my mother was with child, she was forced out of the manor. I revealed myself to Nate once, and announced to him that I was his daughter, but he denied me, and pushed me away. I've had two stepfathers, both hateful men who abused both my mother and the latest was the one who forced me into this deception," she said, starting her story. She told him everything, everything of her time working in the mill, and her mother's sickness. Though she could feel a coldness taking over and a distance building between them, it was cathartic to finally be truthful with him about everything that she had been holding in. When her story was finally over, she stood in front of him, a chill taking over her body that she refused to acknowledge, awaiting his judgement, no matter how painful it would be.

"I knew you weren't Hattie," he said finally, his face so stony she couldn't tell what he was thinking, but her heart leapt with hope upon hearing that he knew she wasn't the young mistress of the house. Did that mean that his heart was still open to her, if he hadn't immediately informed her father?

"You knew?" she asked, breathlessly.

"Yes, of course I knew. We could not talk as intimately as we have without truly knowing each other. Only I didn't know *you*. I only knew that you were not Hattie. I have great sympathy for you, given the difficult position you were put in by your stepfather. And I pity your mother, still living under his thumb, sick as she is. You need not worry, I will not reveal your secret to your father, or anyone else for that matter. But I cannot, in good conscience, continue with our courtship."

Her heart sank, and a panic rose within her. She didn't know what her life looked like without him in it, and she wasn't sure she could continue without his company.

"Please, please, don't give up on me because of what is not in my control. I did not choose to come here, the choice I was given between taking my mother's place in her marriage bed or come here was an impossible one. My hand was forced, please don't think any differently of me. Nothing that has passed between us up to this point has been a lie, my feelings for you are true! I've never been dishonest in my affection. Getting to know you has been the only honest part of my time here in this cursed manor! Tell me what I can do to win back your trust," she begged.

"Nothing. There's nothing you can do. You say it was not your choice, but have you given a single thought as to what became of the true Hattie? People have stopped looking for her, and she may still need our help. But you've been concerned with only yourself.

Besides, how would it look if I continued our courtship, we got married, and then the truth was revealed? My family would be ruined, and my father is right. I ought to be thinking of my family more than I do. I need to stop being so selfish, and consider those outside of myself. Perhaps you ought to do the same," he said, leaving the umbrella with Eva and walking back towards the manor.

"Luther, please!" she said, running after him, but it was no use. He left abruptly, without saying so much as another word to her. The devastation sunk into her bones.

Once he'd returned home, Luther marched to his chambers, pacing around the room. His heart was crushed. He'd hoped that it would be easy to leave once he'd heard the truth, and the cruelty of her deception was revealed, but that hadn't been the case at all. He had been moved by the pain in her story, and it took all the strength he had to leave her standing there in the rain. She had suffered so much, so much more than he could ever understand. But it didn't change the fact that they could no longer pretend. Their courtship had to end, and any hope of a future for the two of them was hopeless.

It would be difficult to explain to his father why he'd ended things. His attachment to Hattie was the last thing in his life that his father approved of, and now that was ruined as well. He had no choice: he'd have to give up his painting and start working for his father immediately. It would be the only way he would be forgiven for spoiling the potential marriage between his house and the Morris family. He felt angry with Eva for making him fall in love with a facade, and for causing him so much pain now. Despite this ire, he still longed to be with her, and wished he could protect her, if only from a distance. She had changed him for the better and giving up his art for the sake of keeping her secret was a worthy sacrifice.

Chapter 4

She'd had to tell him eventually, though she waited as long as possible to, until the very last moment. Nate was bound to find out from someone that Luther had ended their courtship, and it would be best if he heard the news from her. The conversation did not go well, although he didn't hit her, as she'd grown to expect angry men to do.

"What did you do to ruin it? How did you spoil it? Have you been spending too much time reading all these books and not paying enough attention to him? He's been here every day for the last week, so I don't understand what could have gone wrong!" Nate said, standing up in his office, angrily leaning against the mantle.

"I don't know," Eva said crying. She couldn't come up with a viable reason for Luther to have called off their acquaintance, so she opted for ignorance instead.

"He must have given you some reason girl. Think! Perhaps he can be convinced to see reason. I know his father had as high hopes for the match as I did."

"I don't know," Eva repeated. "He said something about how he didn't think he could love me," she lied.

"Nonsense, what does love matter in these affairs? You clearly shared some kind of affection for each other, wasn't that enough? I certainly didn't love your mother when I married her, but she was pleasing to me, and came from a good family. It's the artistic side of him speaking, it must be. The painting, it must have given him a romantic affliction. There's no cure for that kind of absurdity. He'll regret this when he wastes away his fortune. A fortune he could have doubled by marrying you. Well, the loss is his. We'll see what other eligible bachelors I can find for you. There must be someone who will marry you and take you off my hands."

The next two weeks dragged on, without a single note or word from Luther. Eva was truly on her own now in the giant manor. There were friends who came to call, but she refused to see anyone, nervous that someone else would be able to see through her charade the way that Luther had. She considered running away again, but feared some kind of vicious reprisal from Byron, inflicted upon her mother. Her days were spent reading, pining over Luther, missing her mother, and trying to stay as quiet as possible, as if invisibility was the answer to her existence. There was no way out for her, but also no way forward.

For better or worse, all that changed when Nate called her into his office one day. She wasn't sure why, but part of her suspected it might be because he'd found another suitor for her. Eva was hardly ready to entertain another man, but it was bound to happen sooner or later.

Nate looked dangerously calm when she entered his study. She had grown accustomed to his endless rants, and his quiet stoicism made her nervous. Worse even than that, was the fact that he wasn't alone. There was another man there, older than her father, and looking equally serious in his long, black cloak and white kerchief crossed about his neck. Nate did not introduce him.

"Sit down," he said, and waited to speak again until she did.

"What can I do for you, Father?" she asked, and he chuckled.

"There's no need to keep up the charade any longer, child. I've received a letter this morning. Do you know who it was from?" he asked, looking at her. Her heart started beating quickly. Had Luther written to him, informing her father of her deceit? He'd promised he wouldn't, but perhaps he'd thought better of it.

"No," she responded quietly.

"No, of course you wouldn't. Well, let me tell you. It was from a business acquaintance of mine who frequently trades in Scotland. On a recent trip, he swears to me that he ran into my daughter. My daughter Hattie. I thought that couldn't possibly be true because my Hattie is right here with me! But I read on. It seems that *my* Hattie ran away a little over three weeks ago, with her lover, the dastardly Mr. Chelten. They are now married and staying with his family in Edinburgh while they plan their return to Yorkshire. Needless to say, I am beyond shocked by Hattie's behaviour, but that is neither here nor there. There were no roadside bandits after all, and I've now paid a thousand pounds to a man for doing nothing at all. And you, you little piece of scum, you tricked me and took advantage of my charity, wearing my daughter's dresses and sleeping in her bed. Make no mistake, you will not see the outside of a jail cell for the rest of your life. Take her away, I can't abide the sight of her," Nate said dismissively, gesturing for the man Eva now registered as the magistrate to take her away.

"No, please, Father, have pity on me! I was forced into this deception, I promise you it was not of my own making!" she screamed, but it was no use. She was thrust into the back of the magistrate's carriage, her hands tied behind her back.

The next few hours passed in a blur. She tried to tell anyone that would listen that they needed to arrest Bryon Adams, that he was the one responsible for the deception, but not a single person would listen to her. She couldn't stop her tears which were relentless. What was to become of her mother now? She'd gone from one cage to another and both had prevented her from being able to take care of her mother. But now, any hope she'd ever had of seeing her again disappeared. She would waste away here, while her mother wasted away in her sick bed, underfed and mistreated by her cruel husband. Just the night before she had been crying about a boy and now, all concerns of that nature felt a thousand miles away. The cold cell that was her new home echoed with her cries long into the night.

***

"It seems you were wise after all, calling things off with the Morris girl. Did you hear the news?" Luther's father, George, said to him the next afternoon.

"What do you mean?" Luther asked, suddenly worried for Eva's well-being. He had thought about her every second of every day since he'd last seen her and simultaneously spent the same time trying to think of anything else. The memory of her haunted him, and he longed to be cured of his lovesickness. Despite this desire, he clung to his father's words, anxious for news of her.

"It seems that we were all deceived. The girl who presented herself as Hattie after her ordeal with the bandits was not Hattie at all, it was her half-sister, the product of an affair Nate had many years ago. The real Hattie is married now, to some charlatan merchant, Mr. Chelten. This must all be quite shocking to you, but I must apologise. I believe your instincts were to be trusted, in this regard at any rate. Why is it that women succumb to these shameful deceits? It's truly disgraceful. You've saved our family's name, by distancing yourself from that devil of a girl," George said, casually sipping on his afternoon tea. Luther couldn't believe his father's heartless tone.

"What's become of her? The girl? Where is she now?"

"In the jailhouse, of course, where she belongs. Where else should she be? The real question is how do I proceed with my acquaintance with Nate Morris? He is a friend but we can't be seen to be…"

Luther stood up abruptly, leaving without saying another word to his father. George looked after him, confused, shrugged, and went back to sipping his tea.

Galloping toward Longford Manor, Luther tried to work out his next move. He needed to talk to Nate Morris, convince him to drop the charges against Eva, and come to her defence. The last thing that girl needed in her life was more mistreatment after she'd already suffered so much. He was ashamed to think of how callously he had left her when really he should have helped her. As a prominent member of Yorkshire society, his word held quite a bit of sway, and he might have worked with her to find a way to come clean. Her stepfather was the man who ought to be in a jail cell, not Eva.

"I implore you, I'm begging you, sir, have some pity for your daughter. She's lived a difficult life, made even more difficult by your lack of empathy for her," Luther said when he finally got an audience with Nate Morris.

"That little imp of a girl? Luther, come to your senses! You escaped what might have been a ruinous connection with her. Leave me in peace to pick up the pieces of my reputation. I deserve your empathy, not that vagabond of a girl and her tramp of a mother," Nate said, dismissing Luther's request that he forgive Eva.

"You brought her into this world, and now you deny her your mercy because of the struggles she suffered at your hand? This could be your opportunity to mend your bond with her. You've already lost one daughter who couldn't live up to your harsh standards, and now you stand to lose another," Luther argued, feeling himself overstep boundaries, but not being able to hold back. Nate did not take it well, and his face grew red with rage.

"Do not for one moment think that you can tell me how to treat my daughters. The both of them are insolent, selfish girls who have thought only of themselves, without considering for a moment the consequences of their actions. Get out of my house before I have you removed!" he shouted, and Luther knew he'd lost the battle.

If Nate wasn't going to take a stand for his daughter, Luther would have to step in himself. Getting back on his horse, Luther knew what he had to do.

Chapter 5

He knew the magistrate was a cold, judgmental man. Irvine's reputation preceded him, and though Luther had never met the man, he was sure the ordeal ahead of him would be equally as challenging as the one he'd just left. He'd have to manage his arguments better than he had with Nate Morris.

"I've come to discuss the case of Eva Price. It's come to my attention that she has been incarcerated here?"

"Indeed she is. What did you wish to discuss on the subject?" Magistrate Irvine asked coldly, hardly looking up from the ledger in front of him.

"I would like to plead for her freedom. I am aware that she was caught going by a false identity, but she was forced into the ruse, and it was her stepfather, Byron Adams, who is to blame for the whole undertaking," Luther said, trying to keep an even tone. Logic is what would appeal to a man like Irvine.

"I am aware of the accusation, but Byron Adams is a contributing member of society, and a man of good repute, taken in by the wayward girl, and talked into the ludicrous plan. Eva, on the other hand, is nothing more than a vagabond, desperate for another man to leech off of. Don't be taken in by her. We spoke to Byron, of course, and he explained the whole tale."

Luther was speechless, stunned by the heartlessness of the magistrate. He had a sneaking suspicion that Byron had bribed the man to avoid further penalty. If he could get away with that, then so could he. Breathing deeply to dispel the anger in his heart, Luther spoke the language that he knew Irvine would understand - that of money.

"I am willing to pay whatever it takes to secure Eva's freedom. She has behaved very badly, and the court will be expecting some kind of retribution. I can think of no better way of repaying her debt to society than by serving her with some kind of fee - that I will fulfill for her," Luther said calmly. Irvine looked up at him, working out the offer in his head. The magistrate knew that Luther was a wealthy man, and whatever price he placed on Eva's head, Irvine himself would be able to take at least half of it for himself.

The rest of the conversation went very quickly, and they settled on a number. It was a hefty fine, but Eva's freedom was worth every penny to Luther.

***

"Miss Price!"

The voice of the magistrate came ringing out after the lock on Eva's cell clanged open.

"Yes?" she answered weakly, simply wanting to be left in peace.

"Your release has been negotiated. Follow me, and hurry now," he said, and Eva's eyes opened wide. Her release? Who would have argued on her behalf? Had her father come to his senses? Timidly walking out of her cell, exhausted after her ordeal, she shuffled after the magistrate, only to see Luther Ward standing in front of her. She almost fainted with surprise.

"Eva," he said, coming towards her and taking her by the arm. That's when she really did faint.

Waking up hours later, she was in a strange room, in a strange bed. It had a pleasant smell, and the sheets were soft. Opening her eyes, she saw Luther seated beside the bed, book in hand. He sat up as soon as he saw that she was awake, full of questions as to her well-being.

"You're awake! How are you? Do you feel faint still, or dizzy?"

"Where am I," she asked, finding her voice.

"We're at the Hotel. I apologise that I couldn't take you home with me, but my father wouldn't have approved. I've had some food brought up, if you're hungry at all," he said gesturing towards a small table on the other side of the room.

"I'm all right, thank you. I'm so sorry for putting you out like this," she said, pulling herself up, and wondering how she looked. In truth, she looked terribly pretty, or at least, that's what Luther thought. The colour had returned to her cheeks, and her hair was framing her face beautifully. "I hate to ask yet more of you, but I must, on behalf of my mother. She's still trapped and ailing with the man who is to blame for most of my misery. I fear that she may die if she doesn't get help soon. She needs a good doctor, but more than anything she needs to be freed from the clutches of that man. Please, I beg of you to help her. I swear to you, you'll never have to see me again, and this is the last request I'll ever make of you. Please," she said, feeling the faintness coming back to her head.

Luther took her hand in his and smiled.

"Dearest Eva, you haven't put me out at all. On the contrary, it is to you that I owe an apology. You told me your story of struggle, and I abandoned you when I ought to have helped you. And I hope to never let you down again, not for the rest of my days. Of course I will help your mother. We'll find her the best doctor in the whole county and make sure that she is brought back to health."

"Do you mean that, Luther? After all that I have done, after all the lies that I have told, you are still willing to help me and my mother? It is more than I deserve," Eva said, comforted by his hand on hers.

"I do mean it," Luther said, laughing and smiling at the delirious woman. "And I mean more than just that. Eva Price, since the very first day I met you, my heart has been yours. I knew instantly that you were not Hattie, but I couldn't bring myself to confront you, as it meant that I would no longer be able to spend time with you. I ache for you when you're not near. I was inconsolable after that day that I broke off our courtship. What I felt for Hattie could never compare to what I feel for you, and I should have recognised my feelings for what they were earlier - love. I love you, Eva Price, and I never want to go another day without you. Can you forgive me for giving up when I did, and could you make me the happiest man in all of Yorkshire and agree to be my wife?" he asked, and Eva could feel his hand shaking.

Her own breath quickened, and words failed her. *I must be dreaming,* she thought. *I'll wake up in a few minutes, back in that jail cell and all this will have disappeared.* She pinched herself, but the room stayed where it was. Luther stayed where he was, his disheveled, curly hair making him appear even more dashing than usual.

"Say something Eva, please," he said, and Eva realised that she still had not responded to his marriage proposal. It was all too good to be true, and she couldn't believe what she was hearing, but it was true, and she was going to have to think of something to say. Nothing she could think of would accurately describe her feelings, or how much she loved him too.

"Yes, Luther, yes, of course I would like to marry you. I would love to marry you! I have never loved another, I've never felt anything even approaching love for another man, and I would be the luckiest woman in the whole world to wake up next to you every day. But I can't let you ruin yourself like this for me. I have no money, even less than no money. Your reputation would be ruined, and your father would never forgive you. You've already given me so much, I can't let you do this, too," she said, the tears starting to prick at her eyes. As unbelievable as this proposal was, her rejection of it was even more unlikely, and she hated the sound of the words coming out of her mouth.

"Don't say that, Eva, you are the most perfect, thoughtful, funny, beautiful woman I've ever met. If my father doesn't approve of you, I don't approve of my father. We already have all the money we could ever hope for, so why should the fortune of who I love matter at all? Besides, I've been working with my father for about a month now, and I believe his heart has softened towards my desires. If I tell him of my love for you, he'll support me. As to my reputation, tell me, what artist has a lily-white past? If anything, my connection with you will make me more intriguing to the artistic world. All I want to do is make you happy. Will you let me do that?" he asked once more.

The fortress around her heart was starting to crack, and a smile broke through the pain. "Yes. I will marry you Luther Ward. Just promise me one thing."

"Anything, whatever you desire," he said, nodding.

"Promise me that you aren't too good to be true?"

"I swear to you Eva, I will live every day for the rest of my life trying to live up to your expectations of me. To be the man that you deserve," he said.

Eva's heart soared.

***

The next two months were like a dream. Luther immediately made sure that Mary's health was seen to and moved her into the inn with Eva. Their reunion was a sweet one, and the women cried for hours, holding each other and healing their hearts. Her condition was indeed grave, but even one week out of Byron's grasp improved Mary's demeanour. She said it had been awful, with Eva being gone for so long, but forgave her daughter for leaving.

"Everything happens for a reason, and look at how it's all turned out. You've found an angel of a man who will treat you like the princess you were meant to be," Mary said, her fever finally broken. Byron had put up a bit of a fight when they'd gone to take her away, but Luther knew that enough money would calm him down, and it was true. All it took was a bribe, and Mary was as free as a married woman could be.

As soon as they could move her, Luther organised for Mary to live in a small cottage on his estate. He tried to convince Mary to come live with them in the proper estate, but Mary protested that she wasn't meant to live in a big, old house like Rutnell Hall. She preferred a modest life, and the cottage on the grounds would be just perfect for her.

The wedding had been a small affair which some in town thought was rushed, but Eva thought it was perfect. Even her father attended, though she thought his presence there was more to do with a desire to repair his reputation than to show his support for his daughter. George Ward did come around to the match in the end once he met Eva and her mother. It was difficult to find a heart that hardened to the two charming women and seeing how happy his son was brought joy to his own. Luther thought that perhaps he was getting soft in his old age. He took a special shining to Mary, and Eva couldn't help but think that in a different life the two of them might have made a loving match. The sad truth was that Mary would be contractually tied to Byron until the day that one of them died. That didn't stop Mary and George from getting along, and he often spent afternoons with her at the inn together, playing cards and going on short walks about town.

The day came to move into Rutnell Hall, and as soon as Mary was well enough to move, they brought her to her new home.

"I'll be close to you should you need anything at all," Eva said to her mother when they situated her in the cottage. It was a charming house, cosy and warm, with a garden overflowing with wildflowers. The perfect house for Mary. Every day she started to feel better, the country air and peaceful view bringing her fortitude.

"There will be staff to help you with anything you need, Mary. Your wish is our command; you can hold me to that."

"Luther," Mary said, holding onto her new son-in-law's hand, "just promise me that you'll take care of my girl. She's been through a lot, we both have, and she deserves her knight in shining armour. Promise me that you'll be that for her," she whispered, though Eva could hear every word she spoke.

"The only person who wants that more than you is me, Mary. I swear to you, I will take care of her as best I can," he assured her, and they left her to enjoy her home, the first home that had ever truly been hers.

Walking back towards Rutnell Hall, Eva slipped her hand into Luther's. "I never thought all this would be possible for me, Luther. What did I ever do to deserve you?"

"I think you mean what have I done to deserve you, Eva, you have proven to me that the heart is capable of overcoming great injury, and I feel honoured to have a place in yours. Welcome home, Mrs. Ward," he said, pointing towards where the view of Rutnell Hall was appearing, over a green hill, with the sun setting behind it, pink against the puffy clouds. The vista took Eva's breath away. The Hall was stunning, lined with parapets and more windows than she could count, exceeded only by the beauty of the garden. Of all this, she was mistress. The thought all at once terrified and revived her.

Beside her, Luther leaned over, tucking a piece of hair behind her ear, the feeling of his hand on her cheek making her heart skip a beat. With one arm around her waist, and his other bringing her darling face to his, Luther kissed her. It was a deep kiss, one filled with longing, and a promise that said she could dare to dream. She melted into his arms, feeling a love that she hadn't ever thought could be hers.

When their lips finally parted, he tenderly kissed the tip of her nose, followed by her forehead and each cheek, making her giggle.

"I think I have an idea for a painting I'd like to start working on," Luther said, as they started walking towards the Hall.

"Is it of me? Not that I don't like the portrait of Hattie, but I think I deserve my own now," Eva said with a smile.

"Maybe, you'll just have to wait and see!" Luther responded teasingly.

"Don't be cruel to me, Luther! I heard what my mother said to you. You promised to be nice to me, for the rest of your life. Don't tell me you're having trouble already."

"Eva, I can't imagine that I'm ever going to want to paint anyone but you. Today, tomorrow, and forever."

He smiled down at her, the sunset reflecting in her eyes. This day was ending, but their love was only just starting.

The End

Printed in Great Britain
by Amazon